# THE
# Charles Addams
# MOTHER
# GOOSE

## SIMON & SCHUSTER BOOKS FOR YOUNG READERS
New York  London  Toronto  Sydney  Singapore

Many thanks to the Manuscripts Archives Division; the New York Public Library; and Astor, Lenox, and Tilden Foundation for their assistance in creating this book.

SIMON & SCHUSTER BOOKS FOR YOUNG READERS
An imprint of Simon & Schuster Children's Publishing Division
1230 Avenue of the Americas, New York, New York 10020

Book design by Paula Winicur
The text for this book is set in Old Claude.
The illustrations are rendered in TK.
Printed in the United States of America

2 4 6 8 10 9 7 5 3 1

Library of Congress Cataloging-in-Publication Data
Chas. Addams Mother Goose.
The Charles Addams Mother Goose / [illustrated] by Charles Addams.
p.      cm.
Originally published under title: The Chas. Addams Mother Goose. New York:
Windmill Books, 1967.
Summary: Traditional Mother Goose rhymes illustrated  by the cartoonist who created "The Addams Family."
ISBN: 0-689-84874-9
1. Nursery rhymes. 2. Children's poetry. [1. Nursery rhymes.] I. Addams, Charles, 1912- ill. II. Mother Goose. III. Title.
PZ8.3868 Ch 2002
398.8—dc21      2001042849

# FOREWORD

In 1967 Charles Addams created his own twist to the time-honored tales of Mother Goose. I think it was possibly due to a longtime desire sparked by famed bibliophile and *Saturday Review of Literature* cofounder Christopher Morley and his 1942 letter to Random House president Bennett Cerf suggesting he publish an Addams version of the nursery rhymes. Or it could have been due to fellow New Jersey denizen Carolyn Rush and her in-depth studies of Mother Goose, who, when interviewed in 1935 stated, "The rimes we grew to love in childhood have even more interest as we grow older and learn they have historic value." But more than likely, it was because of Charlie's steadfast conviction to enjoy life's lessons through the uncluttered eyes of a child; to ignore convention and have fun with it.

It was in the midst of the war in Vietnam, a time of great uncertainty for Americans, that Charlie chose to underscore an arena familiar to us all—Mother Goose. But he gave us a new way to view it, poking fun at the sometimes incredibly frightening events of the rhymes. My own children squealed at his updated versions. How wonderful to find a dinosaur inside Humpty Dumpty, rather than worrying that he had fallen and couldn't be repaired. Or being reassured that the old woman who lived under the hill had all the comforts of a real home and was better for it. And, of course, deciphering that nothing short of a witch could be stirring up a cauldron of something as awful as pease porridge!

In all of his work, Charlie found humor in every character and situation he drew, no matter how wicked or eccentric they were. In some cases, he softened the fright, while in others he gave it an edge, both of which made us laugh. Therefore, I am very pleased that his book is being reissued as a deluxe edition that includes a drawing, which was omitted from the original version, as well as work and photographs taken from Charlie's lifetime. It is the perfect time for us to enjoy *The Charles Addams Mother Goose* all over again.

Chas Addams died in September of 1988. Were he still with us, this would read: "Thanks to my good friend, Kevin Miserocchi, who did all the work and made this book possible. C.S.A."

Mrs. Charles Addams
Sagaponack, New York
31 October 2001

Humpty Dumpty sat on a wall;

Humpty Dumpty had a great fall.

All the king's horses and all the king's men
Cannot put Humpty Dumpty together again.

Three blind mice, see how they run!
     They all ran after the farmer's wife,
Who cut off their tails with a carving knife.
     Did you ever see such a sight in your life
As three blind mice?

Little Miss Muffet
Sat on a tuffet,
Eating her curds and whey.
There came a big spider,
Who sat down beside her
And frightened Miss Muffet away.

Tom, Tom, the piper's son,
    Stole a pig and away did run;
The pig was eat, and Tom was beat,
    Till he run crying down the street.

One misty, moisty morning,
    When cloudy was the weather,
There I met an old man
    Clothed all in leather—
Clothed all in leather
    With cap under his chin.
How do you do, and how do you do,
    And how do you do again?

There was an old woman
        Lived under a hill,
And if she isn't gone,
        She lives there still.

Pease porridge hot,
Pease porridge cold,
Pease porridge in the pot nine days old.
Some like it hot,
Some like it cold,
Some like it in the pot nine days old.

Sing a song of sixpence, a pocket full of rye;
    Four and twenty blackbirds baked in a pie.
When the pie was opened, the birds began to sing:
    Wasn't that a dainty dish to set before the king?
The king was in the countinghouse, counting out his money;
    The queen was in the parlor, eating bread and honey;
The maid was in the garden, hanging out the clothes,
    When down came a blackbird and snapped off her nose.

Dickory, dickory, dare!
    The pig flew up in the air;
The man in brown soon brought him down.
    Dickory, dickory, dare!

Hickory, dickory, dock!
The mouse ran up the clock;

The clock struck one,
    And down he run.
Hickory, dickory, dock!

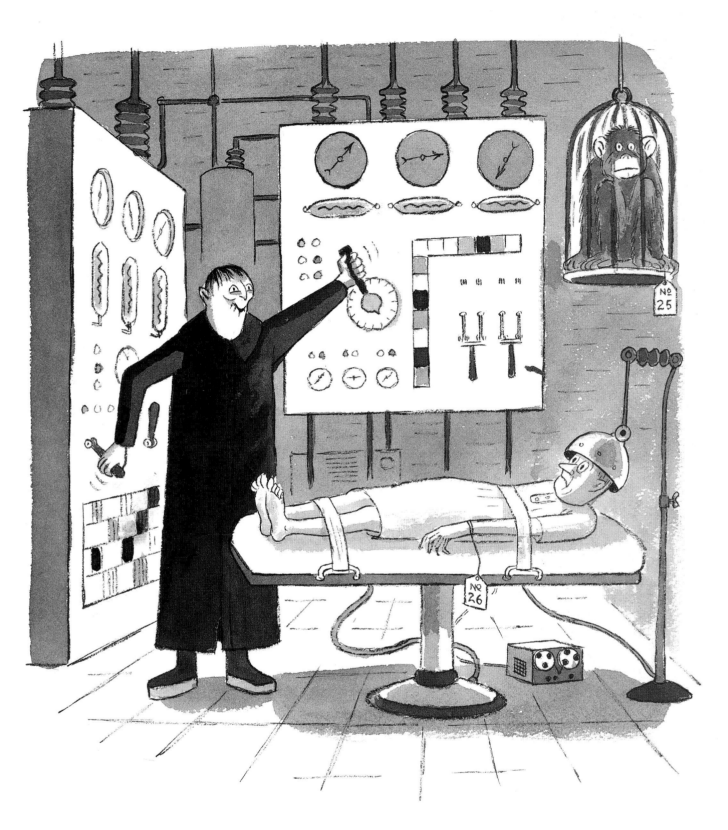

I do not like thee, Doctor Fell;
    The reason why I cannot tell.
But this I know, and know full well;
    I do not like thee, Doctor Fell.

Solomon Grundy,

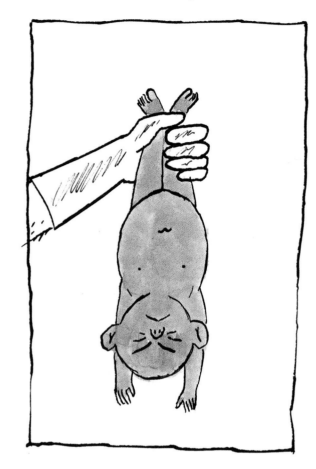

Born on Monday,

Christened on Tuesday,

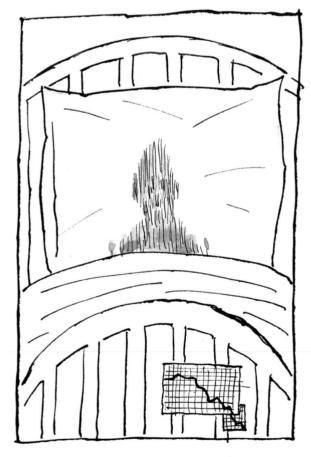

Worse on Friday,

Died on Saturday,

Married on Wednesday,

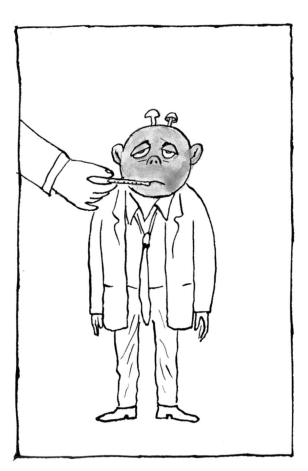

Took ill on Thursday,

Buried on Sunday.

This is the end
    Of Solomon Grundy.

This is the house that Jack built.

**B**

This is the malt
    That lay in the house that Jack built.

**C**

This is the rat
    That ate the malt
That lay in the house
    that Jack built.

**D**

This is the cat
    That killed the rat
That ate the malt
    That lay in the house
    that Jack built.

**E**

This is the dog
    That worried the cat
That killed the rat
    That ate the malt
That lay in the house that Jack built.

**F**

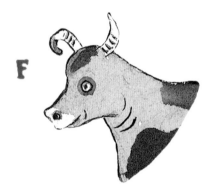

This is the cow with the crumpled horn,
    That tossed the dog
That worried the cat
    That killed the rat
That ate the malt
    That lay in the house that Jack built.

**G**

This is the maiden all forlorn,
    That milked the cow with the
        crumpled horn,
    That tossed the dog
        That worried the cat
    That killed the rat
        That ate the malt
    That lay in the house that Jack built.

**H**

This is the man all tattered and
    torn,
        That kissed the maiden all
        forlorn,
That milked the cow with the
crumpled horn,
        That tossed the dog
That worried the cat
        That killed the rat
That ate the malt
        That lay in the house that
Jack built.

**I**

This is the priest all shaven
    and shorn,
        That married the man all
        tattered and torn,
        That kissed the maiden all
        forlorn,
    That milked the cow with the
        crumpled horn,
That tossed the dog
        That worried the cat
That killed the rat
        That ate the malt
That lay in the house that Jack built.

**J**

This is the cock that crowed in the morn,
    That waked the priest all shaven
    and shorn,
That married the man all tattered and torn,
    That kissed the maiden all forlorn,
That milked the cow with the crumpled horn,
    That tossed the dog
That worried the cat
    That killed the rat
That ate the malt
    That lay in the house that Jack built.

**K**

This is the farmer sowing his corn,
    That kept the cock that crowed in
    the morn,
That waked the priest all shaven and shorn,
    That married the man all tattered
    and torn,
That kissed the maiden all forlorn,
    That milked the cow with the
    crumpled horn,
That tossed the dog
    That worried the cat
That killed the rat
    That ate the malt
That lay in the house that Jack built.

Little King Pippin he built a fine hall,
    Pie-crust and pastry-crust that was the wall.
The windows were made of black pudding and white
    And slated with pancakes, you ne'er saw the like.

Girls and boys,
     Come out to play,
The moon does shine
     As bright as day.
Come with a hoop,
     Come with a call,
Come with a good will,
     Or not at all.

Mistress Mary, quite contrary,
    How does your garden grow?
With silver bells and cockleshells
    And pretty maids all in a row.

Rain, rain, go away,
    Come again another day.

St. Dunstan, as the story goes,
    Once pulled the devil by the nose
With red hot tongs, which made him roar,
    That could be heard ten miles or more.

Fishy, fishy in the brook,
    Daddy catch him on a hook,
Mommy fry him in a pan,
    Johnny eat him like a man.

There was an old woman tossed in a basket,
 Seventeen times as high as the moon;
But where she was going, no mortal could tell,
 For under her arm she carried a broom.
"Old woman, old woman, old woman," said I,
 "Whither, oh whither, oh whither so high?"
"To sweep the cobwebs from the sky,
 and I'll be with you by-and-by."

Jack Sprat
    Could eat no fat;
His wife could eat no lean.
    And so, betwixt them both,
They licked the platter clean.

Bat, bat,
Come under my hat,
And I'll give you a slice of bacon;
And when I bake,
I'll give you a cake
If I am not mistaken.

Pretty John Watts,
    We are troubled with rats;
Will you drive them out of the house?
    We have mice too in plenty
That feast in the pantry,
    But let them stay
And nibble away.
    What harm is a little brown mouse?

As I was going to St. Ives,
    I met a man with seven wives.
Each wife had seven sacks,
    Each sack had seven cats,
Each cat had seven kits.
    Kits, cats, sacks, and wives,
How many were going to St. Ives?

Here am I,
    Little Jumping Joan;
When nobody's with me,
    I'm all alone.

Wee Willie Winkie
    Runs through the town,
Upstairs and downstairs
    In his nightgown,
Rapping at the window,
    Crying through the lock,
"Are the children all in bed,
    For now it's eight o'clock?"

Old Mother Goose, when
    She wanted to wander,
Would fly through the air
    On a very fine gander.

# THE
# Charles Addams
# MOTHER
# GOOSE
# SCRAPBOOK

*Chas Addams*

Charles, circa 1912–1913

Charles, age twelve, with his mother, Grace. His father, Charles H. Addams, is hiding in the bushes.

The "original" Addams family, circa 1922–1923

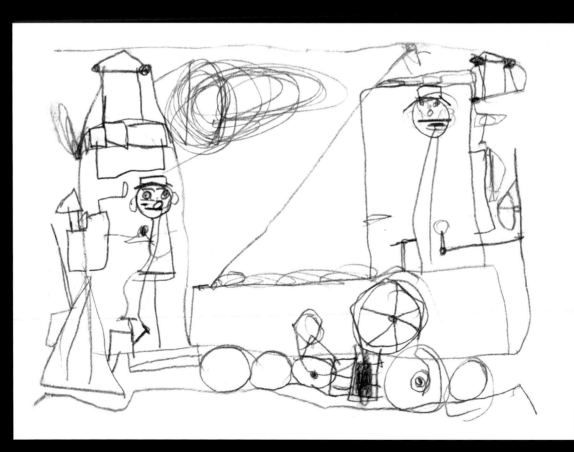

Already a burgeoning artist, Charles, at age four, loved everything to do with trains and engineering—monsters would come later.

Quite the collector, Charles posing
with his assemblage of medieval crossbows.

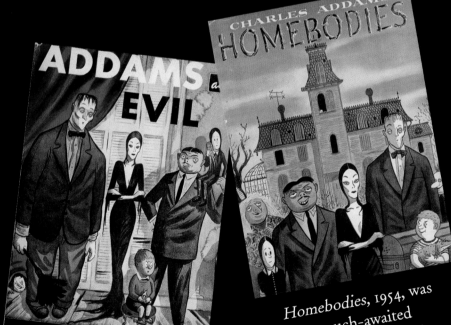

Charles's first book, Drawn
and Quartered, was published
with much acclaim in 1942
and then later reissued, as
seen here, in 1962.

Addams and Evil, 1947, was
the first book to fully
integrate the characters that
would later become known as
"The Addams Family."

Homebodies, 1954, was
a much-awaited
follow-up about this
most unusual family.

Other classics by Charles Addams:

MONSTER RALLY

1950 (reissued 1970)

NIGHTCRAWLERS

1957

MY CROWD

1970

BLACK MARIA

A NEW CARTOON COLLECTION

1960

THE GROANING BOARD

1964

FAVORITE HAUNTS

1976

Creature Comforts

1981

Charles with the "aboriginal" dolls,
Wednesday and Pugsley Addams.

A red sky at night is a shepherd's delight
A red sky in the morning is a shepherd's warning

Charles and his dog, Alice B. Curr

THE NEW YORKER

Oct. 30, 1989
THE
NEW YORKER
Price $1.75